SCARLETT AND SAM

SEARCH
FOR THE
SHAMIR

by Eric A. Kimmel

illustrations by Ivica Stevanovic

KAR-BEN
PUBLISHING

FOR JONAGOLD RAVEN

KAR-BEN PUBLISHING
A division of Lerner Publishing Group, Inc.
241 First Avenue North
Minneapolis, MN 55401 USA
1-800-4-KARBEN

Website address: www.karben.com

Additional photo: © minik/Shutterstock.com.

Main body text set in Janson Text LT Std 13/20.
Typeface provided by Adobe Systems.

Library of Congress Cataloging-in-Publication Data

The Cataloging-in-Publication Data for *Search for the Shamir* is on file at
the Library of Congress.
ISBN 978-1-5124-2937-4 (lib. bdg.)
ISBN 978-1-5124-2938-1 (pbk.)
ISBN 978-1-5124-2939-8 (eb pdf)

LC record available at https://lccn.loc.gov/2017000776

Manufactured in Hong Kong
1-44375-34619-5/25/2017

011823.4K1/B1159/A8

CONTENTS

CHAPTER 1
BUGS AND BUTTERFLIES

"Hey! There's one! Over by Grandma Mina's dahlias!" Sam called to Scarlett.

The twins were outside in the garden, working on a science project they'd signed up for online. They were taking part in a butterfly count sponsored by the science museum. Children all over the city had volunteered to spend two hours on this specific afternoon counting the different species of butterflies they could identify.

You could look for butterflies anywhere outside—in a yard, a park, or even a vacant lot. The challenge was to identify them. That way, entomologists—scientists who study insects— could compare the count with previous years and tell whether butterfly populations were increasing or decreasing.

In Hebrew class, Scarlett and Sam had been studying the idea of *tikkun olam*: caring for the world and the creatures who live in it. That's why they were so eager to help with the butterfly count.

"Where are you looking? I still can't see it," Scarlett called to Sam. She had her cell phone out so she could take a picture of the butterfly as soon as she could get it in the frame.

"It's in there with the orange flowers," Sam said. "It's orange, too. That's why it's hard to see. Wait till it moves."

"There! I see it now." Scarlett took the picture with her cell phone.

"I got a good shot of its wings. That will make it easy to identify later."

Suddenly a scream came from inside the house. "EEEEEEEEK!"

"That's Grandma Mina!" cried Scarlett. "Something's wrong!" She and Sam ran for the house.

They found Grandma Mina in the dining room. Her hand shook as she pointed at the beautiful carpet hanging on the far wall. The carpet had been in Scarlett and Sam's family for generations. It was one of the few things Grandma Mina and her family had been able to take with them when they fled Iran. Grandma Mina always said that the carpet protected them through all sorts of danger. She claimed that strands of magic had been woven into the carpet when it was made.

"Grandma Mina! What's the matter?!" Scarlett shouted.

"Bug! There's a bug!" Grandma Mina's voice

shook. Grandma Mina hated bugs. Scarlett and
Sam couldn't understand how someone who had
faced so many real dangers—and who loved to
garden—could be afraid of bugs. But it didn't
matter if it was a butterfly or a ladybug. If it
belonged to the insect family, she wanted it *gone*!

"Where is it?" Sam asked.

"There! On the carpet!"

"I'll catch it and take it outside," said Sam.
He didn't like to kill anything: spiders, moths,
even flies.

"I'll get a jar," said Scarlett, who felt the same way.

Scarlett grabbed an empty peanut butter jar
and handed it to Sam. They walked slowly around
the dining room table as they approached the
carpet. They didn't want to frighten the bug.
If it took off, they might have to hunt for it all
over the house. If it took off in Grandma Mina's
direction, they might have to hunt for *her* all over
town.

Sam carried the jar and Scarlett held the lid. The plan was to get the jar over the bug, put the lid on before it got out, and release it in the garden. The twins didn't see much of a challenge. They'd been doing this for Grandma Mina since they were little.

"I see it!" said Scarlett.

"Whoa!" Sam exclaimed. "What kind of bug is that?!"

This was clearly no ordinary insect. The bug was the size of a small banana. Its eyes were on stalks, like a slug's or snail's. On its back was a pair of dragonfly wings.

"It's no butterfly, that's for sure," Sam said.

"Go slowly," whispered Scarlett. "Don't hurt it. I want to take it to the science museum when we catch it. I'll bet someone there can tell us what it is."

"Unless it's a new species. Then we'll get to name it after ourselves."

"No, you won't! You'll name it after me!" Grandma Mina called to them from a safe spot way across the room. "I'm the one who nearly had a heart attack. I don't care where you take that creature. Just get it out of the house."

"Slowly . . . slowly . . . don't move, little buggy . . ." Sam whispered.

"You mean *big* buggy," Scarlett said.

"Almost . . . quick! Bring the lid!" Sam cried as he placed the jar over the bug. Just then the patterns of the carpet started spinning.

"Oh, no! Here we go!" Scarlett cried as the living room began to whirl.

CHAPTER 2

SLINGS AND STONES

The whirling slowly stopped. The twins looked around. "Where did the carpet take us?" asked Sam. Wherever they were, it was a place with lots of hills. Some were as tall as small mountains. Scarlett and Sam found themselves standing on one of them.

From their vantage point, they could see a city surrounded by a high wall. A jumble of small buildings jammed close together around a tangle of tiny streets. Sam pointed to a large building. "That's probably city hall," said Sam.

"Or some kind of palace," Scarlett suggested.

"Shouldn't a palace be in the middle of the city?"

"Not if it has to leave room for something more important. Look!"

Scarlett pointed to a huge mesa rising up from the city's center. There was nothing on the mesa, though. The great, flat rock was bare.

"Weird that it's so empty," murmured Sam. "Shouldn't there be a palace, a fort—something—up there?"

"Add that to our list of questions," Scarlett said. "Along with 'Where are we?' and 'Why are we here?'"

"Only one way to find out anything," said Sam.

Scarlett nodded. "Let's go."

Scarlett and Sam made their way down the hill. They followed a path that led them through several small villages. The people seemed friendly. A few waved. Most were busy looking after flocks of sheep or working in the fields and garden plots clinging to the hillsides.

A small group of boys and girls about their age began following the twins as they walked along.

The boys carried long sticks that were curved at the end. "They must be shepherds," said Sam. "Whenever you see shepherds in Bible storybooks, they're carrying sticks like that."

"Where are the sheep?" said Scarlett.

"Beats me. Maybe these shepherds are taking a break."

"Hey, you two! Who are you? Where are you from?" demanded a tall boy who appeared to be the leader. The other children gathered behind him, giggling and pointing at Scarlett and Sam.

"Don't be afraid," one of the girls added. "We won't hurt you."

"Unless you're a Moabite. Or a Philistine," one of the smaller boys said. A few boys stuck out their chests, trying to look tough and brave.

"Don't listen to them. We won't hurt you as long as you come in peace," the tall boy said. "Everyone who comes in peace is welcome in Jerusalem."

"Jerusalem!" Sam whispered to Scarlett. "So that's where we are."

"Yeah. But when?" Scarlett whispered back. "Jerusalem's more than three thousand years old. That's a lot of history."

"We'll find out," said Sam. He spoke to the children. "If that's Jerusalem, you must be Hebrews."

"Of course!" the tall boy said. "Welcome! Are you Hebrews too? What tribe are you from?"

"What do you mean?" asked Scarlett.

The children looked puzzled. "Everyone in Israel belongs to one of the twelve tribes," the tall boy said. "We're mostly from Judah and Benjamin around here. Zebulon's people live over by the coast. You'll run into Dan and Gad if you go farther north . . ."

"He's talking about the Lost Tribes of Israel," Sam whispered, amazed.

"But they aren't lost yet," said Scarlett. "They're still in the area. I think I have an idea of where and when we are."

The tall boy asked, "What are your names?"

"I'm Scarlett."

"And I'm Sam."

The boy tapped his chest. "I'm Gideon. I'm named after my ancestor. He was a great hero."

"We know," Scarlett said. "He defeated the Midianites. We learned all about that in our Bible class."

"Where are you from?" Gideon asked.

"The United States," Sam answered.

"Never heard of it," another boy said.

"It's far away," Sam explained.

"Farther than Babylon?" a girl asked. "We once met a man who rode his camel all the way from Babylon."

"Way farther," said Sam.

"But we're glad to be here. We're looking forward to meeting . . . King David," Scarlett said, taking a guess as to who might be sitting on the throne.

The children stopped smiling. "You're too late. King David's dead," the tall boy told her. "His son Solomon is king now."

"Oh," said Sam. "That's cool too! Though I was hoping King David would teach me how to play the harp."

"Nobody could play like King David," the tall boy said. "But if you want to learn to use a sling, I could teach you. Here, Gabi. Hold my crook." He handed his curved stick to one of the smaller children. Then he took a braided cord from his belt. Scarlett and Sam saw that the cord split in the middle for about three inches. One end ended in a loop. The boy picked up a smooth round stone. He tucked it into the split. Placing the loop around his middle finger and holding the other end between this index finger and thumb, he began whirling the stone around in a clockwise direction.

He whirled it three times, took a step forward, and let it go. Scarlett heard a snap like a whip cracking. The stone smacked into the top of a distant hill as if it had been shot out of a cannon.

"Wow!" Sam and Scarlett exclaimed.

"Anyone who looks after sheep knows how to use a sling," one of the girls told Scarlett. "David wasn't always a king. He was a shepherd when he was a boy. We have to protect our lambs from wolves and foxes. Sometimes even lions. All sorts of wild animals roam these hills."

"Now I see how King David was able to bring down that giant, Goliath," said Sam.

"That wasn't what made David great," Gideon said. "Hitting a giant with a sling is no great feat. How can you miss? Every shepherd I know can hit a rabbit on the run. What made King David great was having the courage to stand in the open and let the giant get close enough so he could hit him with the full force of the stone. King David had one shot. If he'd failed to bring down the giant, we'd all be slaves to the Philistines. David's courage made him a great king. Everyone in Israel misses him."

"But Solomon's king now," pointed out Scarlett. "He's just as great as his father was."

Gideon and the other children looked away, suddenly embarrassed.

"Keep going down this road," Gideon told the twins. "It will take you to the city gate. You can see it from here." He handed his sling to Sam. "You saw how I did it. Twirl it front to back. Keep your eye on the target. The rest is practice." He motioned to one of the other boys. "Give Scarlett your sling, Ya'akov. I'll make you another." To Scarlett he said, "You try too. Girls can handle a sling as well as boys."

The twins thanked the children, who said goodbye and walked back to their village.

"That was strange," Sam said. "I can see why they miss King David. But they sure weren't excited about King Solomon. I don't get it. Who wouldn't be excited about being ruled by the wisest man in the world?"

Scarlett picked up a stone to try out her sling. "Good question. Something isn't right. Maybe that's why we're here."

"What do you mean?" asked Sam.

"The carpet didn't send us back in time to shoot rocks at rabbits," Scarlett said. "There must be something more important that we're supposed to do."

Sam frowned. "What do you think it is?"

"I don't know yet," Scarlett said. "Let's keep walking. My guess is we'll find out when we get to Jerusalem."

CHAPTER 3
THE PROPHET

Scarlett and Sam tried out their slings as they followed the road to Jerusalem.

"I think I'm getting the hang of this," Sam told Scarlett. "See that bush? Bet I can hit it." He pointed to a dead shrub halfway up the nearest hill. Then he picked up a stone, fitted it to the sling, and whirled the sling around the way Gideon had shown him. Once he had enough momentum, he released one end of the cord.

The stone went flying up the hillside.

"Lucky you're not facing Goliath. You'd be toast," said Scarlett as the stone kicked up a plume of dirt ten feet from the bush.

"Yeah? Let's see you hit it," said Sam.

Scarlett picked up a stone and sent it hurtling from her sling. It hit a bit closer than Sam's, but not much.

They shared a laugh. "Neither of us is a David," said Sam.

"Not yet anyway," Scarlett said.

They tucked their slings away as the track they were following widened. Soon it became a road. The road turned into a highway as they came closer to the city.

Scarlett and Sam weren't the only ones heading to Israel's capital. Throngs of people filled the route to Jerusalem. The twins made their way past shepherds driving flocks of sheep and goats to market. Adding to the noise and dust were long caravans of camels bringing goods from distant lands. The camels opened their jaws and roared. That scared the sheep and goats, who began baaing and bleating. The goatherds and shepherds started yelling at the camel drivers. The camel drivers yelled back.

It looked as if a fight might begin, but just then a troop of soldiers happened to march by. *Tramp. Tramp. Tramp.* The soldiers wore leather and carried spears. Their commander rode in a chariot. "Make way! Clear a path!" the soldiers shouted to the crowds.

The twins walked on, following the soldiers. Along the way they ran into puppeteers, storytellers, musicians, fortune-tellers, a magician, pie and candy sellers, and a man with a trained monkey. It seemed the whole world was on its way to Jerusalem.

Moving along with the crowd, Scarlett and Sam soon found themselves at the towering gates of the city. Guards at the checkpoint questioned everyone.

"State your names," the guard said. This fellow was clearly no-nonsense and very much in charge. He stood well over six feet tall. He had a clipped beard and wore a dented helmet with a tall, horsehair crest on top. His iron breastplate was also full of dents. No doubt, this man had seen plenty of action. A sword hung at his side.

"I'm Scarlett," Scarlett said.

"And I'm Sam," Sam added.

"Where are you from?"

"The United States," Sam stammered.

"Where's that?" the guard snapped. "It better not be near Moab. There's been trouble on the Moab border. We have orders to detain all Moabites."

Scarlett shook her head. "We're not from Moab. We don't even know where Moab is."

"Trying to be funny? I'll let that go." The guard glowered down at them from under his helmet. "What's your business in Jerusalem?"

"Well, we don't really know why we're here or what we're supposed to do," said Sam.

"Hmm," said the guard, narrowing his eyes. "You don't know why you're here. I think I know why. You're spies! And you're under arrest!" The guard turned to a group of soldiers standing inside the gate. "Bring the chains!"

Before the twins could protest, someone called, "Wait!"

Scarlett and Sam turned to see who was speaking. It was the strangest person they had ever seen. He looked like a ball of hair with arms and legs sticking out. Thick, matted dreadlocks hung to his shoulders. His beard, equally thick and matted, hung past his waist. He wore a tunic, cloak, and sandals made from goatskins, just as hairy as the rest of him.

"These are the two I told you to watch for," the hairy man told the guard. He turned to the twins. "Scarlett and Sam, right?"

"Uh . . . yeah!" Sam stammered. "Who are you? How do you know our names?"

"Easy," the man replied. "God told me."

Scarlett and Sam gave each other a sideways glance. Maybe they should take their chances with the guard. Or just turn around and run.

"I know it sounds weird," the hairy man said. "But you have to believe me. God *does* talk to me. I'm a prophet. I'm Nathan. Maybe you've heard of me."

"Nathan the Prophet!" Sam whispered to Scarlett. "He was a good friend to David and Solomon."

Scarlett held her nose. "If he's a prophet, maybe God could tell him to make friends with a bar of soap."

"I think he's okay," Sam said. "He wants to help

us. Plus, I bet a dungeon wouldn't smell any better than he does." He turned to Nathan. "So God told you about us?"

"That's right. God spoke to me the other day while I was tending my goats. God said that two young visitors named Scarlett and Sam would come to Jerusalem from a distant land. They'd help us solve all our problems."

"What sort of problems?" Scarlett asked.

Nathan laughed. "Solomon can tell you better than I can. Let's go. He's waiting for us. And he needs all the help he can get."

"King Solomon?" Scarlett asked. "But he's the wisest man who ever lived," Scarlett said.

"Well, we're working on that," said Nathan.

CHAPTER 4
THE HOLY MOUNTAIN

Scarlett and Sam followed Nathan through the gate into the streets of the densely packed city. People approached the prophet from all directions. They clutched Nathan's hands, begging for a blessing.

"Prophet, help me have a child!"

"Prophet, make my business prosper!"

"Prophet, I'm sick. The doctors cannot help. Cure me, I beg you!"

"Prophet, let my husband return safely from his journey!"

"My children, I cannot bless you," Nathan told the people over and over again. "All blessings come from God. A prophet has no special powers. I am an ordinary man—a humble goatherd. I will remember you in my prayers. I hope that you will do the same for me."

"If prophets don't have special powers, what makes them special?" Scarlett asked.

"Only that we try to be truthful," Nathan said. "I can't predict the future like fortune-tellers say they can. I can't pull rabbits and pigeons out of the air like magicians. I hear voices speaking to me from inside my head. I know in my heart that they come from God because everything the voices tell me is kind, true, and just. That means I must do what the voices say. Sometimes it's scary. Many times, I've had to go before King David and tell him something he'd done was wrong and that

God was displeased with him. You never saw King David get angry. I'd rather walk into a lion's den. But I knew I had to tell the king the truth because that's what God wanted me to do and that's how I could help the king. I loved God more than I feared David. And I loved David enough to risk his anger. I guess that's what makes me a prophet."

By then they had arrived at the *shuk*, the vast covered market where everything from sheep to spices was being sold. The people haggling in the market stalls came from every corner of the world.

Nathan pointed. "The men over there are Phoenicians," he told the twins. "They're great sailors. Their ships travel to all parts of the earth. Hiram, their king, was a good friend of King David. I'm hoping he'll be a friend to Solomon. The ones with the felt hats are Medes. They come from the mountains of Persia. Those people are Ishmaelites . . . let's see, those are Sabeans . . . Elamites . . . Nubians . . ."

A troop of soldiers marched by. These men looked different from the guards at the gate. They were taller and clean-shaven. Some wore crowns of feathers on their heads.

"Who are they?" asked Sam.

"Philistines and Cretans," Nathan explained. "Cretans are great soldiers, among the best in the world. They served King David. Now they serve Solomon. At least for the time being."

"What do you mean?" asked Sam.

"The Cretans are mercenaries. They'll fight for anyone for pay. If Solomon can't pay them, they'll go back to Crete. Or fight for someone else."

"What about the Philistines?" said Scarlett. "I thought they were Israel's enemies. King David fought them, and King Saul before him. So did Samson."

"You know about Samson? That was such a long time ago," Nathan said

"We know lots of things," said Scarlett.

"I see that," Nathan said. "Well, then you know the Philistines are formidable fighters, too. They came here from across the Great Sea and chased us up into the hills—where we might have stayed, except for King David. He didn't just kill their best fighter, Goliath. He figured out their weakness."

"What was that?" Scarlett asked.

"The Philistines could never unite as one people," Nathan explained. "Their cities had their own kings who spent most of their time fighting each other. The Philistines grew weaker as Israel grew stronger. Finally, David gave them a choice: either join Israel as allies or be wiped out."

"I get it," said Sam. "He made them an offer they couldn't refuse."

"Ha! Exactly! I'll have to remember that," Nathan said. He continued. "King David was tough enough to keep Israel's enemies in line. Now everyone's wondering if Solomon can do the same. Solomon has a lot of problems. He looks to me for answers. He has no one else. I do my best, but I can't tell him what to do if God doesn't tell me. That's where you come in."

"Us?" Scarlett and Sam said together.

"You have the answers," said Nathan.

Scarlett and Sam stared at each other. Answers? They didn't even know the questions.

But at least they had a guide. Not a single street in Jerusalem went straight. There were no maps, no street signs, no names or numbers on any of the buildings.

"No one would ever find you if you got lost here," said Sam.

"Wow! Look!" Scarlett suddenly exclaimed. The alley they were following suddenly opened onto a vast open space. Scarlett and Sam stared up at the huge rock towering over their heads. Its steep sides leveled off to a form a wide plateau.

"Now I know where we are," added Scarlett. "That's the mesa we saw from the hillside."

"That's the most famous mountain in the world," Nathan told them. "Mount Moriah. Haven't you heard of it?"

Scarlett nodded. "I remember now! It's in the Torah. That's where Abraham went to sacrifice Isaac."

"And at the last moment God sent an angel to save Isaac's life," added Sam. "You mean that happened up there, Nathan? On top of that rock?"

"That's right," Nathan said. "And that's not the only important thing to happen there. Some say this is where Creation began—where God said, 'Let there be light' and separated water from dry land. This mountain is a holy place. It belongs to God. Nothing can ever be built on it unless it's for a holy purpose."

Scarlett looked up at the bare, gray rock. "Like what?"

Nathan smiled. "You'll see."

CHAPTER 5

IN SOLOMON'S COURT

Nathan led the twins around the base of the mountain and onto a crowded plaza. Soldiers stationed every few yards kept the people moving. Looking up, Scarlett and Sam saw a large building made of blocks of white stone. More soldiers looked down from the walls and towers.

"This must be the palace," Sam said.

"It is!" Nathan pointed to the structure with pride "The grandest building in Israel. King

David started on it after he captured Jerusalem. Before that, our kings moved around too much to need a permanent home. King Saul spent most of his time in a tent. David said that if Israel were going to be a proper kingdom, its king needed a proper home. What do you think?"

Scarlett and Sam smiled politely. They couldn't bring themselves to tell Nathan what they really thought. After all, they had seen Pharaoh's palace in ancient Egypt and taken several trips to Disneyland. By comparison, this place looked like a garage.

Nathan started walking across the plaza. The soldiers saw him coming. "Make way for Nathan! Make way for the prophet of God!" they cried. That's when someone in the crowd noticed Scarlett and Sam. People started yelling.

"It's them! The miraculous twins! They've arrived!"

The soldiers tried to push the crowd back, but there were too many people.

Suddenly Nathan raised his hands high in the air. "Get back, everyone! Be quiet! I'm getting an important message."

The crowd backed away just enough for the soldiers to hustle Scarlett, Sam, and Nathan across the plaza and through the palace gate.

"That was intense," Sam said as soon as he could catch his breath. "What message did God send you, Nathan?"

"I never said I was getting a message from God," said Nathan. "I told them I was getting a message. And I was, loud and clear: We'd better get out of here before this mob tears us apart. Just because I'm a prophet doesn't mean I have to wait for God to tell me what to do. God wants us to think for ourselves. Now let's go see the king."

***

Scarlett and Sam began getting messages of their own as they followed Nathan to the throne room. None of them were good.

"This place is in trouble," Scarlett whispered to Sam.

"I'm getting the same vibe," Sam replied.

The royal palace of Israel definitely needed redecorating. The carpets were worn and full of holes. The tapestries on the wall were frayed. Sunflower seeds littered the floor. Heaps of trash sat in corners.

None of the guards seemed to care. They waved people through the checkpoints without questioning or searching them. A few had the nerve to demand bribes.

Nathan shook his head. "Disgraceful! It wasn't like this in David's time."

"Maybe Solomon has a looser style," Scarlett suggested.

"No. People respected David. They don't

respect Solomon," Nathan replied. "And time's running out."

"What does that mean?" Sam whispered to Scarlett.

"It means they're looking to us for answers," Scarlett said.

"Got any?" snorted Sam.

"Not yet."

***

Scarlett and Sam followed Nathan into the crowded throne room.

"That's Solomon?" Scarlett gasped when she saw the young man perched on the rickety chair that was supposed to be the royal throne. "He looks like he got pulled off the street and dressed up in a king costume. That crown's too big. And that ratty robe reminds me of Grandma Mina's bathrobe. Except Grandma Mina would have given a robe like that to Goodwill."

Sam shrugged. "Don't be too hard on him. He probably has bigger things to worry about." Solomon definitely needed a royal makeover. But for now, Sam was less interested in what Solomon was wearing than in what he was doing.

Solomon was judging the people. From the size of the crowd filling the throne room, Sam guessed that there were a lot of people who needed judging.

Two women stood before the king, shouting at each other. One of them held a crying baby, which the other woman kept trying to snatch away.

"Let me see if I've got this straight," the king said solemnly. "You live next door to each other."

"Unfortunately," snarled one woman.

"And you each gave birth to a baby on the same day. One baby, sadly, died, and the baby who survived . . ."

"Is mine!" snapped the first woman.

"No, he's mine!" cried the other woman.

Solomon gazed thoughtfully at the two women until they fell silent—along with the rest of the crowd, which had been chatting, gossiping, spitting sunflower seeds all over the floor, and pretty much ignoring the king.

Solomon stood up. He pointed at the women. "Since you can't agree who's the mother of this child, I'm going to take a sword and cut the baby in half. You'll each get a piece of him. That's fair, isn't it?"

The first woman started screaming. "No! Oh, Your Majesty! I beg you! Let her have the baby. Don't hurt my child!"

The second woman remained silent. "Do you have anything to say before I pass judgment?" Solomon asked her.

The woman shook her head. "You are the king. What must be, must be."

"That's all I need to hear," said Solomon. "The

first woman is clearly the real mother. She would rather have her baby taken away than see the child harmed. Give the baby to her."

The woman took the baby and ran from the throne room, weeping with joy.

Solomon turned to the second woman. "Do you know what I'm going to do with you?" he asked.

The woman shook her head. Scarlett and Sam could see her trembling with fear and sorrow. Solomon lowered his voice. He spoke to her gently.

"I'm not going to punish you. I know you're grieving for your baby. I will make sure your baby has a proper burial. But you will not leave here with your hands and your heart empty. There are so many children in Jerusalem who have no mother or father. Can you find a place in your heart for such a child?"

The woman began weeping. "Yes! Yes, O Solomon!" she cried. "I can!"

"Then we will help you find one to love as your own."

As Solomon's servants led the woman away, Sam whispered to Nathan, "That was amazing! Solomon's brilliant. Why does he need us?"

"You'll see," said Nathan.

Solomon sat back on his throne. "Next case," he said, sounding exhausted.

Nathan called from the back of the room, "Solomon! I have important news. The twins we've been expecting. They're here!"

Solomon's mouth dropped open. It was hard to tell if the look on his face showed joy or surprise. Maybe both. "Clear the room!" he commanded. "I have important things to discuss with the twins. The future of Israel depends on it."

CHAPTER 6
ROYAL HEADACHES

King Solomon's private audience chamber was
nothing like Scarlett and Sam had imagined.
No silk hangings. No soft cushions. No servants
with ostrich plume fans. No delicacies or sweet
drinks cooled with snow from the mountains.
The chamber was more like a closet, and it was
as threadbare and shabby as everything else in
the palace.

There weren't even any chairs, just a low bench

built into the wall. A flowerpot held a long-dead plant. Solomon's royal robes hung on pegs. There were only three pegs. Solomon only had three robes and he was wearing one.

Solomon invited Nathan, Scarlett, and Sam to sit down on the bench. He called down the hall for someone to bring refreshments.

A servant showed up carrying a tray. Her shawl was on crooked. The hem of her skirt was coming loose.

She set the tray on a low table. There was a pitcher of some kind of juice that tasted like weak Kool-Aid, and a platter of cookies that looked rather sad and stale.

"Is that all?" Solomon said. "These are important guests."

The servant shrugged. "Take it or leave it. That's all we have. By the way, when am I going to get paid? I have kids to feed, you know."

"I'm working on it," Solomon said apologetically.

"Work harder," the servant snapped on her way out the door.

"Sorry about that," said Solomon to Scarlett and Sam.

"That's okay," said Sam. "These cookies look delicious." Sam tasted a cookie. One bite was enough. He looked around for a place where he could politely ditch it.

The king sighed. "Just spit it into the flowerpot. It's all right, I don't like them either. But my servant is right. It's all we have."

"I don't get it," said Scarlett. "You're a king. You're the son of David, the mightiest king in Israel's history. How can you be so poor that you can't even afford decent cookies?"

Solomon hung his crown on the one empty peg. "Didn't Nathan tell you? David's time is past. This is a new age and it's not a good one. Israel's broke."

"We figured," said Scarlett. "But how did that

happen?" The king rubbed his forehead and began to explain.

***

Solomon's Story

Our people have been fighting one enemy or another since the days of Joshua. But after my father, David, became king, we defeated most of our enemies. Even the Philistines gave up and asked to become our allies.

You'd think we'd be grateful for our victories and God's blessings. No way! Instead of enjoying the fruits of peace, we began quarreling among ourselves. That's when the real trouble began.

I'm the baby, the youngest in our family. My older brothers started fighting over who should be the next king even before our father was dead.

Dad was so sad about that. He knew he was growing old. He wanted me to become king after him, but I was still a little boy. How could a little boy rule over Israel?

Dad tried to stay alive as long as possible for my sake. He had heard that a person wouldn't die while studying Torah. So my dad studied the Torah day and night. He didn't eat. He didn't sleep. He studied, studied, studied. But in the end, it didn't save him.

And while Dad had been studying, nothing else got done. Debts piled up. Nobody received their wages. By the time Dad died and I took over, the treasury was empty.

Our allies know we're in trouble. Fortunately, the army has stayed loyal—but for how long? Soldiers won't fight if we can't pay them. Hiram, the King of Phoenicia, has been lending us money. That's what's kept us going.

I didn't want Dad's legacy to crumble on my watch. But the only thing I could think of to do was to pray for God's help. I begged God to give me the wisdom to be a good king.

***

"I know the rest," Scarlett said. "God spoke to you and said, 'Solomon, because you asked for wisdom instead of wealth and power, I will give you wealth, power, *and* wisdom. For what is wealth and power without the wisdom to use them properly?'"

"Where did you hear that?" Solomon asked.

"In our Hebrew class."

"Well, don't believe it." Solomon looked around the room. "Wealth? Power? Wisdom? I don't see any."

"Wisdom's definitely here," said Sam. "We saw the way you handled those two women with the baby. That was awesome."

Solomon turned away. "I'm glad you both think I'm wise. But I know better. All the wisdom I have is sitting over there." He pointed to Nathan.

"Who, me?" Nathan said. "I'm just a goatherd."

"You're my best friend," Solomon said. Tears came to his eyes. "I don't know what I'd do without you. Except you've given me my biggest problem yet."

"What's that?" Scarlett asked.

"Tell her, Nathan," Solomon said.

CHAPTER 7
THE SHAMIR

Nathan helped himself to a cup of juice and a cookie before speaking. They were probably better than whatever he got to eat out in the wilderness. Nathan combed the cookie crumbs out of his beard as he spoke.

"A temple. The message came through loud and clear. No mistake about it. God told me he wants Solomon to build a temple."

Solomon got up and began pacing around the

room. "Can you believe that? No money in the treasury! The people ready to revolt, enemies closing in. And God says, 'Build a temple.' How? With what?"

"Now wait a minute . . ." Nathan began.

"No! Tell Scarlett and Sam the rest."

Nathan shrugged. "It's not as crazy as it sounds."

"Let Scarlett and Sam decide. Tell them."

"Well," Nathan began, "we can't use any iron tools to build the Temple. No chisels. No hammers. No crowbars. Not even a nail."

"Why not?" asked Sam.

"Iron is a metal of war," Nathan explained. "God's temple must be a temple of peace."

"What *can* be used, then?" Solomon wanted to know. "How else can we cut the stones for the building?"

"That's where you come in," said Nathan, smiling at Scarlett and Sam. "What do you think?"

Sam and Scarlett glanced at each other. Then Sam raised his hand. "Maybe we can get a used temple from Egypt. They have hundreds of temples there. Maybe we could buy one cheap, take it apart, ship it over, and put it back together here in Jerusalem?"

Nathan shook his head. "Absolutely not! People worship idols in those Egyptian temples. A temple polluted by idol worship can never be used to worship God."

Scarlett jumped in. "Then how about this? The Egyptians use stone tools. There's plenty of stone here. Let's use it."

Scarlett's idea didn't get any more traction than Sam's. Nathan and Solomon both shook their heads.

"Cutting stone with stone tools takes forever," said Solomon. "It works in Egypt because Pharaoh has thousands of slaves to do the work. It would be wrong to force slaves to build God's house. And we can't afford to pay anybody to do it."

"Well, I give up," said Sam. "If God wants us to build a temple, God has to tell us how to do it. Otherwise, it's not fair."

"Hold on! I just remembered something," said Scarlett. "Maybe God already told us. There's a creature called the *shamir* that can split stones just by looking at them."

"How do you know that?" Solomon asked.

"It was in one of the books in our Hebrew School library," Scarlett answered.

"Then God created it for a purpose," Solomon said. "Could it be to help us build the Temple?"

"There's only one way to find out. Where do we find the shamir?" asked Sam.

"That wasn't in the book," Scarlett said.

"God must know. I'll ask," said Nathan. The prophet stretched out on the bench. He closed his eyes. Soon he was snoring.

"Is he meditating?" Scarlett asked.

"He's asleep," Sam said. "This isn't getting us anywhere."

"Be patient, Sam," said Solomon. "God isn't a servant. We can't summon God whenever we please."

"God doesn't text or send emails," Scarlett added. "We'll just have to wait."

Sam sighed and helped himself to another stale cookie. Scarlett kept her eyes fixed on Nathan, waiting for a sign that some sort of message might be coming through. They waited . . . and waited . . . and waited. Sam ate the last cookie. Solomon poured another glass of juice.

"AAAAHHHHHH!" Nathan yelled and sat up. "Ashmodai has the shamir! ASHMODAI!" He rolled off the bench and fell—*splat!*—onto the floor.

Nathan lay there quivering and jerking for several minutes. Froth bubbled from his lips. Then he lay still.

"Is he dead?" Sam gasped.

Solomon bent over the unconscious prophet. "No, I can feel his pulse. Speak to me, my friend. Without you, Israel is lost."

Behind them, an unfamiliar voice rang out. "That's not true. Israel is never lost. Not as long as God is with us."

CHAPTER 8
SOLOMON'S RING

Scarlett and Sam turned around to see who had spoken. Standing in the doorway was the biggest man the twins had ever seen. He was as tall as an NBA star. They couldn't imagine even Goliath being much taller.

The man wore a chain-mail shirt covered with a bronze breastplate and greaves to protect his legs. He carried his helmet under his arm. It would have scraped the ceiling if it had been on his head. A sword hung from his side. And that wasn't his only weapon. Sam counted four daggers: two on his belt and one strapped to each arm. He was clearly not someone to mess with.

And yet, tough as he looked, the man picked up Nathan and placed him back on the bench with the tenderness of a parent putting a child to bed. "He'll be all right."

"Are you sure?" Sam asked.

"Absolutely. He's a prophet. God won't let harm come to him." The man smiled at Sam and Scarlett. "You must be the twins Nathan told us about. I'm Benayahu ben Yehoiada, captain of Solomon's palace guard."

"That's a mouthful," said Sam.

"You don't have to call me that. Nobody else does."

"What do they call you?" Scarlett asked.

"B.Z. That's short for *barzel*. That means iron. Like this." He flexed his arms. Scarlett and Sam saw his bulging muscles stretching the chain mail.

Scarlett gulped. "I'm Scarlett. That's my brother, Sam."

B.Z. nodded, then asked, "Did Nathan say anything interesting before this happened?"

"We were talking about a creature called the shamir," Scarlett said. "It has the power to split stones."

"Nathan was hoping God would tell us where to find it," Solomon explained.

"I guess that didn't go so well," said B.Z., glancing at the unconscious prophet.

"Yeah," said Sam. "Right before he fainted, he kind of freaked out. He shouted something . . ."

Solomon interrupted. "He shouted, 'Ashmodai has the shamir.' I just hope that isn't true."

Sam saw B.Z.'s weathered face suddenly go pale. "If it is, we have a problem. A big, big problem."

"Who's Ashmodai?" Scarlett asked.

Sam could see B.Z. starting to sweat. He began feeling uneasy himself. What kind of creature was Ashmodai if it could scare a guy as tough as B.Z.?

B.Z.'s chain mail rattled as he wiped the sweat off his face. "Have you heard of Azazel?" he asked Scarlett and Sam.

"Sure!" Scarlett said. "It's in the Torah. We read the parshah about Azazel on Yom Kippur. After they left Egypt, our ancestors sacrificed one goat to God and sent another off into the wilderness— to Azazel. Wherever that is."

"Not where. *Who!*" B.Z. told them. "Azazel is another name for Ashmodai—the king of the demons."

"Demons?!" Sam burst out. "Seriously? How do you know?"

"I heard it from my Ishmaelite friends," B.Z. told him. "Demons inhabit the desert and other wastelands. No one knows the desert better than the Children of Ishmael. They know how to find every oasis, every waterhole. They also know the places to avoid: the rocks, caves, and canyons where demons and evil spirits lurk. Ashmodai inhabits a cave in the side of a mountain they call Jebal al-djinn. That means Demon Mountain."

Solomon did not look convinced. "We can't be sure of that," he said to B.Z. "The Ishmaelites often make up stories to frighten strangers away from their territory."

B.Z. shook his head. "It's no story. I know the Ishmaelites well. I trust them to tell me the truth. They spoke of a man named Hassan who went to explore the mountain. He came back and told his brothers that he had encountered the demon king. Ashmodai lives in a cave halfway up the mountain. He gets water from an old well. A huge boulder covers the well. Ashmodai drinks from it in the morning when he leaves and in the evening when he returns. Hassan suspected a treasure was hidden in the demon's cave, or buried somewhere on the mountain. He told his brothers he was going to return and try to find it. His brothers begged him not to go. Hassan didn't listen to them. He returned to the mountain." B.Z. paused.

"What happened to him?" Scarlett and Sam asked.

B.Z. held out his hands and shrugged. "No one knows. Nobody ever saw Hassan again."

"Now that we know what we're up against, we know what must be done," Solomon said. "Muster all our soldiers. Prepare them for a long expedition across the desert. We'll need camels. Lots of them. How many camels can you gather on short notice?" he asked B.Z.

B.Z. did not look enthusiastic.

"What's wrong?" Solomon asked.

B.Z. bowed low. "O Solomon! You are the king.

I must obey you in all things. However, as a soldier who fought for your father David, I hope you will listen to what I have to say."

"Speak!" Solomon commanded.

"First, our soldiers haven't been paid in months," B.Z. said. "They'd mutiny if I told them they had to march through the desert to fight the demon king. Second, we don't have enough camels for an army that size. Even if we did, the Ishmaelites would never allow such an army to enter their lands. They'd fight us every inch of the way. Finally, what if our army met Ashmodai and was defeated? Remember, his power has no end. He can muster hordes of demons. There's no guarantee that we would win. And there's no escape in the desert. Our soldiers, if defeated, would be wiped out, leaving Israel defenseless. It wouldn't take long for our enemies to close in . . ."

Solomon sat down on the bench and rested his

head on his hands. "What am I going to do? Does anyone have an idea?"

"I do," Sam said, raising his hand. "I saw something like this in a video game. We don't have to fight Ashmodai. All we want is the shamir. What if we put together a special task force to find Ashmodai's cave, locate the shamir, and bring it back? With luck, we can be in and out before Ashmodai even knows we're there."

"That's a good idea—but it's still dangerous," B.Z. said. "I'd go. I could ask my men to come with me. Although, unless we could pay their back wages, I doubt any soldiers would volunteer."

"I would," said Sam.

"So would I," said Scarlett.

"Me, too!" said Nathan, suddenly awake again. He hopped up from the bench. B.Z. had to steady him. "What did I volunteer for?"

"We're going to find the shamir," Sam told him.

"Ashmodai, the king of the demons, has it hidden somewhere in his cave in the desert."

Nathan looked stunned. "How did you figure that out?"

"You told us!" everyone said.

"I did? When?"

"Just now!" said Sam. "You told us that Ashmodai, the king of the demons, had the shamir. B.Z. knows where he lives. That's where we're going. To find the shamir and bring it back."

Nathan gasped. "Ashmodai? I think I'm going to faint."

B.Z. grabbed him before he fell. "You don't have to go."

"No one would blame you if you didn't," Solomon added.

Nathan pulled himself erect, looked the king in the eye, and said, "I'm not afraid. I was just startled. If God sent that prophecy, it means God is with us. And if God is with us, we cannot fail."

***

"It's not too late. I can still go with you," Solomon said.

"You can't take the risk. You're David's son," B.Z. said. "If anything happened to you, it would mean the end of David's line and most likely the end of Israel."

"God can always send another prophet," said Nathan.

"And two more kids," said Scarlett.

"And plenty of soldiers," said B.Z.

"But there will never be another Solomon," Nathan finished.

Solomon sighed. "I guess it's settled, whether or not I like it. Even if I can't go with you, I can make sure you're equipped to face any challenge you meet."

Solomon lit an oil lamp. Scarlett, Sam, and the others followed the king down a dark flight of stairs, into the basement of the palace. Solomon stopped before a heavy oak door studded with nails. He fumbled with the lock. The door swung open. "Where are we?" Sam asked as they stepped over the threshold.

Solomon extended his arm toward the shelves and chests that surrounded them. "This is Israel's treasure room."

"If you have treasure, why do you keep saying Israel's broke?" Scarlett asked.

"Israel's treasures aren't gold and jewels," Solomon explained. "Our real treasures have no price. They cannot be bought or sold. Our treasures are the holy objects that our prophets, judges, and kings have gathered over the centuries. Let me show you some."

Solomon set down the oil lamp. He reached on

top of the shelves and took down a few precious things. One by one, he passed them around so the others could get a look.

"Look, Sam! It's Moses's staff!" said Scarlett.

"And one of the shofars that brought down the walls of Jericho," said B.Z. The huge warrior's hands trembled as he passed the ram's horn to Sam.

"I want to loan you a couple of things for your trip," said Solomon. "They'll help you on your mission."

He bent down and unrolled a bundle resting against the wall.

"It's a carpet!" gasped Sam. He looked closer. The pattern looked familiar even in the dim light. "Scarlett, look! If I didn't know better, I'd say this was Grandma Mina's carpet!"

Scarlett bent down to take a close look herself. "It sure looks like it. How did it get here?"

"I don't know who Grandma Mina is,"

Solomon said, holding the flickering lamp over the intricately patterned rug, "but this isn't really one of the holy treasures of Israel. I keep it down here because I don't want people wiping their feet all over it. It was a gift from the Queen of Sheba. She brought it to Jerusalem when she came to pay her respects after my father's death. It's a special carpet. There's nothing in the world like it."

"What makes it special?" Scarlett asked.

"It flies," said Solomon.

"A flying carpet?" said Nathan. "How does it work?"

"It's very simple. You tell it where you want to go, and it takes you there," Solomon replied.

"This is just what we need!" B.Z. exclaimed. "It'll whisk us to Ashmodai's cave and back again before he suspects anything."

"What are we waiting for?" said Scarlett. "Let's go."

"One moment," Solomon said as B.Z. rolled up the carpet and slung it over his shoulder. "I also want you to have this."

Solomon slipped a heavy, gold ring from his finger. Despite the dim light, Scarlett and Sam could see that a six-pointed star made up of glowing stones was set into the gold band. The gold band was engraved with three strange letters.

"This is the greatest treasure of all," said Solomon. "God made this ring on the sixth day of Creation. Adam was the first to wear it. Noah wore it. So did Abraham, Isaac, Jacob, and Joseph. It was lost when our people went into Egypt. Then God rescued it and gave it to Moses, who gave it to Joshua. From him, it passed to Gideon, Deborah, and Samuel. The prophet Samuel gave it to my father. My father gave it to me, and I now give it to you. The ring controls great powers. Use it wisely and only in emergencies. With this ring on your finger, you will be able to command all living creatures. Including demons."

"Which one of us gets to wear it?" Scarlett asked, hoping she was the one. Her fingers itched to try it on.

"The ring decides," said Solomon. "I can wear it. None of my brothers ever could."

B.Z. tried the ring first. It was far too small to fit on any of his fingers. The same with Nathan. It was huge on Scarlett.

"If it were any bigger, I could use it as a bracelet," she said, slipping it off and handing it to Sam.

It fit perfectly on Sam's middle finger.

"Sweet! I get to command demons!" Sam exclaimed.

"Just don't try to command your sister," Scarlett warned him.

"I think we're ready to go," said B.Z.

"I will pray that God watches over you," said

Solomon as he shut the treasure room door and led them upstairs. "Meanwhile, I'll make sure the building materials are in place and the foundations are prepared. We'll start building the Temple when you get back."

CHAPTER 9

THE KING OF THE DEMONS

They got off to a slow start. The Queen of Sheba's flying carpet wasn't exactly a TIE Fighter out of *Star Wars*. It was more like a Greyhound bus, reliable but slow.

"It beats riding a camel," said B.Z. He'd ridden plenty of those on his trips across the desert. The carpet was a sky-borne raft with plenty of room for passengers and supplies. It carried food, water, thirty feet of iron chain, and a heavy clay jar called an amphora that was as tall as the twins.

"Why are we carrying this thing?" Scarlett asked, pointing at the jar.

"It's part of Plan B. Always have a Plan B," B.Z. explained.

"I don't even know what Plan A is," said Sam.

"Plan A is if everything goes as we hope. Ashmodai probably won't be home during the day. So we might be able to land, find the shamir, and take off again. Ten minutes and we're on our way back to Jerusalem, with the demon king none the wiser. That might work, but only if the shamir is easy to find. If Ashmodai comes home before we finish our search, we'll need a backup plan. That's why we brought the wine."

"What wine?" said Sam.

"In the amphora," B.Z. said. "It's full of expensive Greek wine from Solomon's wine cellar. Plan B is we find Ashmodai's well and pour in the wine. Greek wine is powerful stuff, even mixed with water. When Ashmodai comes home and drinks from his well, he'll fall flat on his face. Down for the count! We'll chain him up. When he regains consciousness, we'll ask him where he keeps the shamir. If he talks, we let him go and take the shamir back to Solomon."

"What if he doesn't?" Scarlett asked.

"Then we take Ashmodai back to Solomon in chains. He's going to hand over the shamir either way."

"Are you sure chains will hold him?" Sam asked.

"They will . . . as long as they're backed up by the power of Solomon's ring," said B.Z.

Sam rubbed the ring and grinned. "I get it now. Good plan, B.Z."

Scarlett agreed. Nathan didn't say anything. He

looked down at the desert passing below, enjoying the ride.

"Any messages from You-Know-Who?" Sam asked him.

Nathan cocked his head. "Nothing so far. I'll let you know if anything comes through."

"Try to give us a warning," Scarlett said. "We don't want you blacking out and falling off the carpet while we're not looking."

"I don't think we'd ever find you again," said Sam. "Everything down there in the desert looks the same. Rocks, sand, more rocks, more sand."

"It's not the same at all," said B.Z. "Not when you really study it. The Ishmaelites can tell you more than I can. Everything's different. They have thirty different words for sand! They can look at a stone, run sand through their fingers, glance up at the stars, and tell you exactly where you are."

Sam glanced at the ring gleaming on his finger.

"I'd doubt we'd be much good at that. I wonder if this ring comes with GPS."

"Let's hope we don't have to try it," Scarlett said.

***

Scarlett and Sam had brought their slings along. They had plenty of opportunities to use them. Whenever they landed the carpet to stretch their legs, the twins used the time to gather stones. B.Z. was an expert slinger. Nathan was no mean marksman himself. Between the two of them, Scarlett and Sam received expert coaching.

"Think of the sling as part of your arm," B.Z. said as he adjusted Scarlett's position. He turned her slightly toward the right, raised her right arm, lowered her left.

"It's like pitching a softball," said Sam, fitting a stone into his sling as he waited for his turn.

"What's a softball?" Nathan asked.

"Never mind," said Sam. Nathan hadn't been kidding when he said he couldn't see the future.

B.Z. pointed at a crack in a nearby boulder. "Pretend that's Ashmodai's cave. There's Ashmodai's head sticking out of it. Let's see you hit him between the eyes."

The twins loaded their slings and sent two stones smacking into the crack at the same time. "Take that, Ashmodai!"

"Good job," said Nathan. "But I hope you don't have to try that in real life. Maybe we'll be lucky and Ashmodai won't be home."

***

They journeyed by day and camped by night. On the fourth day they caught sight of Jebal al-djinn: the Demon Mountain.

"There it is!" B.Z. pointed out a peak looming

over a waste of sand and rock. The mountain itself looked like a crouching demon.

"And that must be Ashmodai's cave." Nathan pointed out an opening in the rock.

"Let's land. We need to scout the terrain," B.Z. said.

"Park by the cave," Scarlett told the carpet. The carpet circled twice and came to a landing.

B.Z. took charge. "Cover the carpet with brush. We don't want Ashmodai to know we're here. Nathan, you'll be our lookout. Call out if you spot anything coming this way. Scarlett and Sam, see if you can find Ashmodai's well."

The twins headed down the mountain. "Let's split up," Sam said to Scarlett. "You go right. I'll go left. Holler if you find anything that looks like a well."

"Will do," Scarlett called back to Sam as she disappeared into the brush.

Sam kept working his way around the

mountainside. Suddenly, he stopped. Ahead, surrounded by clumps of thorn bushes, he saw a wall with a huge stone resting on top of it.

That must be the well, Sam thought. The stone that covered it had to be ten feet thick and twice that in diameter.

Sam doubted that even B.Z., with all his strength, could move that stone. The rest of them were hardly power lifters. All their efforts combined couldn't budge a stone that size. So how were they going to move it?

Suddenly Sam had an idea. Solomon's ring! The ring had the power to command living creatures. Could it move stones? It was worth a try.

Solomon hadn't given Sam any directions for using the ring. Sam couldn't exactly go online to find a how-to video on YouTube. Maybe the ring was like the carpet. You didn't have to say a magic word. You just told it what to do.

Sam decided to give that a shot. The ring must've chosen him for a purpose.

Sam stepped back. Making a fist, he pointed the ring at the stone that covered the well.

"Lift stone!"

The stone began rising into the air. Sam was as astonished by the floating stone as he was by the knowledge that he had caused it to happen. The stone might have floated away altogether if Sam hadn't come to his senses and blurted out, "Stop!"

The stone hung in midair as if suspended by invisible chains.

That's when Sam heard Scarlett calling.

"Sam! Where are you?"

"I'm over here!" Sam called to her. "You have to see this."

Scarlett came scurrying down the mountainside.

"Dude!" she cried when she saw the stone suspended over the well. "How did you manage that?"

"It's Solomon's ring. I commanded the stone to lift . . . and it lifted!"

"You amaze me!" Scarlett told him as they high-fived.

A sudden yell cut their celebration short. Nathan was calling. "Scarlett! Sam! B.Z.! I just got a message. Ashmodai's on his way!"

CHAPTER 10
ASHMODAI

Scarlett and Sam hurried back up the mountain. Nathan met them just as B.Z. came running out of the cave.

"Did you find the shamir?" Sam asked him.

B.Z. shook his head. "If it's in that cave, Ashmodai did a great job hiding it. Did you find the well?"

"Better than that," said Sam. "I used the ring to get the lid off." Sam held up his fist. "Watch this!"

Sam pointed the ring at pile of brush covering the carpet. "Amphora, rise!" Sam commanded.

The amphora rose in the air.

"To the well," said Sam.

The amphora floated down the mountain.

"Faster! We don't have much time," Sam shouted. The amphora flew down the slope. "Now pop your cork and pour the wine into the well."

The amphora did as Sam commanded. As the last drop splashed into the cistern, Sam said, "Disappear!"

The heavy jar vanished.

"Cover the well," said Sam. The stone cover dropped back into place.

"And now we're ready for Ashmodai!" whooped Scarlett. "Let's win this thing!"

"I like your attitude," said B.Z. "Let's find a place to hide. I'll handle Ashmodai when he gets here. The rest of you, be prepared to back me up."

"You got it!" Sam said. "Don't forget, we have the power of the ring."

Nathan corrected him. "We have the power of God, which works through the ring. God's power is the only power there is."

***

Nathan, B.Z., Scarlett, and Sam hid behind some bushes. They waited. And waited. Sam grew impatient. It wasn't just the heat. Why did every fly in the desert seem attracted to him?

"Why don't you use the ring to get rid of them?" Scarlett whispered.

"It doesn't seem right to use one of Israel's holiest treasures to swat flies," Sam whispered back.

Just then they heard a rattling buzz overhead. Scarlett and Sam looked up to see a black shadow circling the mountain.

"It's Ashmodai!" Scarlett gasped.

The demon king landed in front of the cave. Scarlett and Sam lifted their heads above the bushes as much as they dared, hoping to get a look at him. What they saw was more bizarre than terrifying.

The king of the demons was as tall as a giraffe. Like a giraffe, he walked with a herky-jerky motion. He'd take a step and then wait for the rest of his body to catch up with him. Like a buzzard or an eagle, he was clearly more at home in the air than on land. A pair of enormous wings rose from his shoulders. Unlike angel wings covered with downy feathers, Ashmodai's demon wings were sheets of gray skin stretched over a bony frame. They looked like the wings of a prehistoric flying creature.

The rest of him matched the wings: dusty gray skin stretched over bone. He looked as if he had been built out of sticks. His body was all points and sharp angles. A row of spines ran down his backbone.

Ashmodai turned around, allowing Scarlett and Sam to see his face. He had watery blue eyes, a long, thin nose and heavy chin, scraggly teeth and big ears.

"Not as bad as I thought," Sam whispered, hoping he sounded brave. "I've seen scarier demons in video games."

"Yeah, but this one is real," Scarlett whispered back. They both shuddered.

The demon tilted his head as if he were listening for something. Had he heard them? Scarlett and Sam crouched lower behind the bushes. Nearby, B.Z. and Nathan did the same. They all waited to see what Ashmodai would do next.

Fortunately, Ashmodai didn't come in their direction. He turned and started walking down the mountainside path toward the well. Scarlett and Sam watched, amazed, as Ashmodai lifted the heavy stone cover with one hand and set it aside as if it were no more than a pot lid.

"Did you see that?" Sam whispered to Scarlett.

"Don't worry. Remember what Nathan told us. God's on our side. That makes us stronger than any demon," Scarlett whispered.

"I'm not worried," said Sam. Under his breath he muttered, "I'm terrified!"

Ashmodai lowered his head into the well to drink. Suddenly, he yelped.

"GAAAAK!"

Up he came, coughing and spitting. "Awful!" he yelled in a high, screechy voice. "Where's my precious water? Who filled my well with this sludge?"

Sam moaned. "He won't drink it. There goes Plan B. What do we do now?"

"Did you bring your running shoes?" asked Scarlett. She wondered how much time it would take to get to the carpet and fly away. Was the carpet faster than Ashmodai? Judging by how long it took to get from Jerusalem to the mountain, she didn't think so.

Just then they heard, "Ashmodai, by the authority of Solomon, King of Israel, you are under arrest."

B.Z. stepped from behind the rock where he was hiding. He came striding down the slope toward the demon. Ashmodai towered over B.Z. Yet B.Z. didn't even draw his sword. He didn't sound frightened at all. He spoke as calmly as if he were arresting a pickpocket at the Jerusalem shuk.

Ashmodai turned to face him. "Under arrest? I should arrest you for messing with my water supply!"

"No point in hiding now," Scarlett said. "Looks like B.Z. could use some backup."

Scarlett and Sam came out from behind the bushes. So did Nathan.

"Any messages?" Scarlett asked as they walked toward B.Z.

"Nothing so far," Nathan told her. "But I wouldn't worry."

"Why not? That's the king of the demons down there. And he's not happy," Sam said.

"True," said Nathan. "But look. Ashmodai's talking, not fighting. That's a good sign. We're going to come out of this okay."

"As long as we come out of it with the shamir," Scarlett added.

"Who are *these* clowns?" demanded Ashmodai when he saw them approaching. He sounded more irritated than threatening. Sam figured the king of the demons wasn't used to having houseguests.

B.Z. calmly introduced Scarlett, Sam, and Nathan.

"A prophet, eh?" Ashmodai said. "Any messages from You-Know-Who?"

"Not recently," Nathan told him.

"You-Know-Who hasn't spoken to me in eons," grumbled Ashmodai.

"You-Know-Who probably does talk to you," said Nathan. "You just don't listen."

"Why should I?" Ashmodai said. "What's wrong with having a little fun?"

"It's wrong when your fun leaves misery in its wake," said B.Z. "War, plague, famine . . ."

Ashmodai held up his hand. "Don't blame me for all that. I don't force people to fight each other. I don't force them to make others slaves. People make their own misery and blame it on me."

Scarlett and Sam had to admit he had a point.

"Let's get down to business," said Ashmodai. "I've been flying around the world all day. I've been as far as the Land of Gog and Magog. I'm tired and hungry. Now that you've ruined my well with that awful slime, I'm thirsty too. So tell me why you've come here. Was it just to annoy me?"

"Like I said," said B.Z., "King Solomon sent

us to bring you to Jerusalem. You have a choice, Ashmodai. You can come quietly or . . ."

Sam held up his hand. "I have King Solomon's Ring of Power. I can make you do what B.Z. says."

Ashmodai looked startled when he saw the ring. He clearly knew what it was and what it could do. "Let's see if I understand this," he said. "You want me to come with you to Solomon's palace. There I'll have my own room with a soft bed to sleep on. I'll have my meals prepared by the finest chefs in Israel, with plenty of snacks when I want them. I'll have servants to wait on me day and night. I'll be able to read all the interesting books and scrolls in Solomon's library. I can walk around Jerusalem, meeting people from all over the world. Or . . ." he paused. "I can stay in this desert, living in an empty cave on a mountaintop, sleeping on stones, eating bugs and rotten camel meat, drinking stagnant water out of my now-polluted well, with no company except flies. My goodness! I don't know how to choose."

Scarlett and Sam couldn't help giggling.

"What are we waiting for?" said Ashmodai. "Let's go!"

CHAPTER 11

THE HOOPOE

The plan was for B.Z., Nathan, Scarlett, and Sam to land the carpet outside the city and escort Ashmodai through the gates of Jerusalem in the middle of the day. To have the king of the demons led like a prisoner through the streets would be a sure signal to everyone, friend and foe, of the power of Israel's king. *Enemies, beware! If Solomon can subdue the king of the demons, how can you hope to stand against him?*

It was a good plan. Unfortunately, Ashmodai didn't cooperate.

He didn't resist. He didn't gnash his teeth and cry down a thousand deadly threats on Solomon's head.

Instead, he acted as if he were on parade. He made sure to enjoy every minute. He smiled, waved to the people, shook hands, kissed babies.

People ran away at first. However, when they saw he was a friendly demon, they couldn't resist their curiosity and came closer.

"Hey, folks! Good to meet you! How are you doing? Great seeing you! You bet I sign autographs!"

"It's like he's running for president!" Scarlett exclaimed, astonished. Ashmodai had become a superstar. Ten minutes after he walked through the gate he was easily the most popular person in Jerusalem.

"I don't get it," B.Z. muttered. "He's a demon. He causes wars, plagues, misery of all kinds, and laughs about it. How come everybody loves him?"

"That's easy," Sam explained. "Ashmodai's a celebrity."

"What's a celebrity?" Nathan asked.

"It's someone who's famous," said Sam. "You don't have to do anything. You don't have to be talented. You don't have to be smart. You can be the worst person in the world. What counts is that you're famous."

"That's the craziest thing I ever heard. You must come from a very strange land," said B.Z.

"No arguments there," said Scarlett.

It took far longer than they expected to get Ashmodai through the streets and into the palace. "Thank goodness they don't have cell phones here," Scarlett said. "People would have been taking selfies with him every step of the way."

Ashmodai was having the time of his life. That was truly saying something, considering he was as old as Creation.

"I love it here!" he told B.Z. "I think I'll stick around."

They led Ashmodai to the throne room. It wasn't any easier than getting him through the streets. Everyone in the palace dropped whatever they were doing and ran to meet the demon king.

At last, they entered the throne room. Solomon sat on his throne, wearing his crown and royal robes, trying his best to look regally impressive. It didn't work on Ashmodai.

"Hey, Sol!" said Ashmodai. "How're you doing?"

"I'm a king. You're supposed to bow," Solomon said.

"Yeah?" Ashmodai replied. "Well, I've been a king way longer than you have. You should bow to me."

"I'll never bow to a demon!"

"Suit yourself," Ashmodai replied. "I'm hungry. When's lunch?"

Solomon rubbed his forehead.

"Poor Solomon," Scarlett whispered to Sam. "He's getting a headache. I hope it isn't a migraine."

"Ashmodai would give anybody a migraine," Sam replied.

B.Z. spoke up. "If you want lunch or anything else, you have to do what we say."

"Cool!" said Ashmodai. "What do you want? Why did you guys bring me here anyway?"

"We want the shamir," Nathan said.

"Oh, that. I don't have it anymore."

"Stop lying," said Solomon. "We know that God gave you the shamir. We need it to build the Temple. So hand it over."

"I can't," said Ashmodai. "I really don't have it."

"Where is it?" Solomon demanded.

Ashmodai shrugged. "Beats me. God made me give it up a long time ago. God said I was irresponsible. That wasn't fair. It wasn't my fault. I just wanted to see if the thing could really split stones. I had a little accident, that's all."

"What kind of accident?" Scarlett asked.

"Ever hear of the Grand Canyon?" said Ashmodai.

"That's no little accident," said Sam.

"Whatever," Ashmodai said. "I'm hungry. Where's the kitchen?"

B.Z. rolled his eyes. "Down the hall. Follow your nose."

***

Solomon sat on his throne, holding his head. His crown fell off and rolled across the floor. No one bothered to pick it up.

"I can't stand it," Solomon moaned. He banged his fist against his forehead. "What's the matter with me? I'm doing my best. Why doesn't anything go right?"

"I think you need a hug," said Scarlett. She and Sam went up to the throne and put their arms around Solomon. B.Z. and Nathan followed.

"Feel better?" Nathan said.

Solomon sighed. "I just don't understand why God told Nathan that Ashmodai has the shamir, when he really doesn't."

"We'll get to the bottom of this," said B.Z. "Don't give up, Solomon."

"God could be testing us," said Nathan. "God might want to see if we're worthy of possessing the shamir."

B.Z. straightened up. "You may be right, Nathan. God tested Abraham by asking him to sacrifice Isaac, his son."

"God tested Joseph too," Sam added. "His brothers sold him into slavery in Egypt. Even when terrible things happened to him, Joseph never stopped believing in God."

"Same with Deborah," Scarlett said. "She never doubted that God would lead Israel to victory over their enemies, even when the men didn't think it could happen. That's why God gave that victory to the women. They passed the test while the men scored zero."

Sam turned to Scarlett. "Remember when we were at the Red Sea with Moses?" Sam whispered. "The sea didn't split until we started walking into the water. Nothing happened until the Israelites showed their trust in God."

"You haven't failed, Solomon," said Nathan. "It's a test for you. It's a test for all of us. We're in this together."

"Right," agreed B.Z. "We may not know where the shamir is, but we know where it isn't. Ashmodai doesn't have it. So where can it be?"

"We have the flying carpet," Scarlett pointed out. "We could travel anywhere, looking for clues."

"Egypt has vast libraries," mused Solomon.

"And the whole continent of Africa is full of all sorts of animals," B.Z. said.

"Now we're cooking," said Sam. "Nathan, what do you think?"

Nathan didn't answer.

"Nathan, is something wrong?" Scarlett asked him. The prophet stared into the distance. His entire body started shaking.

"He's having a prophecy," said Sam. He and Scarlett caught Nathan just before he fell. Together they sat him down on Solomon's throne. Nathan shivered violently.

"Maybe we should call a doctor," Scarlett said.

"He's in God's hands," Solomon said. "All we can do is watch and wait."

"And let him know that we're here," said Sam. Sam took Nathan's right hand and held it in his own. B.Z. took the left. Scarlett and Solomon each placed their hands on Nathan's shoulders.

A few minutes later, Nathan's body relaxed. He opened his eyes.

"Any messages?" Solomon asked.

Nathan took a breath and began to speak. The words came out in ragged gasps, as if he had just run a marathon.

Nathan shook his head. "Just . . . one . . . word . . ."

"One word? Is that all?" said Solomon.

"It must be important," said Scarlett. "What word was it?"

Nathan took another deep breath. "Du . . . khen . . . fat . . ."

"What?" said Sam.

Scarlett shrugged. "Beats me. Du-khen-fat."

"Wait!" Solomon said. "I know what that means. Dukhenfat is the name of a bird."

Scarlett looked doubtful. "I never heard of a dukhenfat bird. What does it look like? How far do we have to go to find one?" She was not looking forward to another flight across the desert.

Sam's thoughts ran the same way. "Maybe we can find one that's close," he said.

"We can find one that's very close. There's a nesting pair of dukhenfats in my garden," said Solomon. "Another name for the bird is 'hoopoe.' It has a pinkish-brown body, black-and-white wings, and a pinkish-brown crest with black spots. It's about the size of a thrush."

"How big is a thrush?" Sam asked Scarlett.

"I guess it's about the size of a robin. They have different birds here."

Solomon went on, looking more excited than they'd ever seen him. "You'll never forget the hoopoe once you've seen it. I watch the birds every day from my window when I have breakfast. They've built a nest in a hole in the garden wall."

By this time Nathan was starting to recover. "The hoopoe is the key!" he cried, sitting up. "The birds are guarding the shamir."

"How does that make sense?" Sam asked. "The shamir is a bug. Birds *eat* bugs."

"Let's not overthink it," said Solomon. "God wouldn't have left the shamir in their keeping if it wasn't safe with them."

"I'll bet they're more trustworthy than Ashmodai, at least," added Scarlett.

"And we don't have to fly to the end of the earth to find them," said Solomon. "Let's start by checking out the nest in my garden."

"Good idea!" said B.Z.

"Let's go!" said Nathan.

"Wait for us!" said Scarlett and Sam. And off they went.

They didn't notice the rustling of the throne room curtain or the dusty-gray figure sneaking down the corridor, following in their footsteps.

CHAPTER 12
GLASS

Solomon stopped before they reached the wall. He motioned them to hide behind a spreading rhododendron bush.

"Do you see the crack on the top of that wall? The nest's in there," Solomon said. He spoke in a whisper so as not to alarm any birds.

Sam, Scarlett, Nathan, and B.Z. waited with Solomon, eyes fixed on the wall.

"When will the birds come back?" Scarlett

asked. She was getting tired of standing. Bugs were biting her, and the rhododendron oozed icky sap that stuck to her skin.

"Be patient. Birds arrive when they're ready, not when you're ready," Solomon told her.

"You sound like a bird-watcher," said Sam.

"I am!" Solomon said.

"So am I," said Nathan. "I get to see a lot of birds and other animals when I'm up in the hills with my goats." *No wonder*, Scarlett thought. Nathan's beard probably made a fine lining for bird nests.

"Shhh! Everybody get down," said Sam. "I see a hoopoe."

The bird landed on top of the stone wall. It was a hoopoe, all right. Its black-and-white wings and the prominent crest on its head were unmistakable.

"What a beautiful bird!" Scarlett exclaimed. "I wish we had binoculars."

"What's that?" asked B.Z.

"Everybody, shhh!" said Solomon. "We don't want to scare it away."

However, the hoopoe showed no sign of having heard them. Sam saw that it carried something in its beak. Too thick to be a worm. Maybe a caterpillar?

"I hope that's not the shamir," said Sam.

"I doubt it," said Solomon. "God gave them the shamir to safeguard, not to eat." They watched as the hoopoe hopped over to the crack at the top of the wall. It circled the crack, calling, "*Hoo*-poe! *Hoo*-poe!"

"I see something in the crack," said Scarlett. Sure enough, the baby birds were stretching out their heads, demanding food. The hoopoe darted its head in and out of the nest. The chicks grabbed at the caterpillar with their beaks, tearing off big chunks, swallowing them, and cheeping for more. Soon the caterpillar was gone. The hoopoe flew away. The baby birds withdrew into their hidden nest in the crack.

"Wasn't that great? Don't you just love watching things like that?" Solomon truly did have a bird-watcher's soul. Scarlett and Sam had never seen him so happy. Sam was happy, too. Watching the hoopoe had given him an idea.

"Listen up, everybody. What do you think of this?" The others listened as Sam explained his plan.

"What if we covered the crack with a piece of glass? That way, the hoopoes could see their babies, but they couldn't get to them. If they got freaked out enough, they'd use the shamir to cut through the glass. We'd have a chance to grab it and all our problems would be solved."

B.Z. looked doubtful. "I don't see how a glass vase or pitcher would be big enough."

"I'm talking about a flat piece of glass," Sam explained. "Something like a windowpane?"

B.Z., Solomon, and Nathan gave him blank stares.

"What's a windowpane?" Solomon asked.

"Sam," whispered Scarlett, "they don't have glass windows. That's why Solomon's palace is full of flies and insects. They don't have windowpanes to keep them out."

"Why would you put glass in windows?" B.Z. asked.

"I'll explain later," said Sam. He turned to Solomon. "Do you know a glassblower, a bottle maker, someone who works with glass?"

"I do!" said Nathan. "He has a shop and workspace in the shuk."

"Let's send for him," said Scarlett. "We'll need his help."

***

The glassblower was beyond thrilled to be invited to the royal palace. When Nathan brought him before Solomon's throne, he bowed low.

"Forgive me, Mighty King! I am but a humble craftsman. I am unworthy to be in your presence."

"Not true," said Solomon gently. "We need your help. I hear you're an expert with glass."

"I am," the glassblower said. "Would you like me to make a perfume bottle? A flower vase? Some clever glass animals? People always like those. They're my top sellers. I can make a camel, horses . . ."

"Actually," said Sam, "we just want you to make a flat piece of glass. About so big." Sam held his hands about twelve inches apart.

The glassblower looked puzzled. "That's all? Why?"

"Never mind why," said B.Z. "Can you do it?"

The glassblower scratched his head. "I suppose so. I could blow a glass bubble and flatten it out."

"How long would it take?" asked Nathan.

"A few hours. The glass has to cool properly. Otherwise, it might shatter."

"Perfect," Solomon said. "Bring it here when it's done."

***

The glassblower returned late in the afternoon, carrying a parcel wrapped in a sack. He bowed before Solomon. Then he opened the sack and took out a round disk of greenish glass about the size of a dinner plate. It certainly would not have won any awards in an art show. It was lumpy, misshapen, and full of bubbles. But it would cover the crack in the wall.

As they carried the glass disk out to the garden, Solomon remarked, "If that guy could make more of these, we could put them in some kind of frame and put them over the palace windows. That would let light in but keep the bugs out. What do you think?"

"What wisdom!" B.Z. exclaimed. "Let's work

on it after we find the shamir and get the Temple built."

Scarlett winked at Sam. "Don't look now. I think we just invented windowpanes."

***

Solomon, B.Z., Nathan, Scarlett, and Sam entered the garden, carrying the disk. Solomon checked to make sure the hoopoe parents weren't nearby. Carefully, he placed the glass disk above the crack in the wall. It covered it completely. The hoopoes would be able to see their nestlings. They just wouldn't be able to get to them.

Everyone hurried back to the hiding place behind the rhododendron. This time they didn't have to wait long. Within minutes, they heard a familiar cry.

"*Hoo*-poe! *Hoo*-poe!"

The mother and father birds flew in at the same time. One carried another caterpillar. The other had a large beetle. The baby birds began chirping. Sam could hear them from where he stood.

"Peep! Peep! Peep!"

"*Hoo*-poe! *Hoo*-poe!"

The two adult birds pecked at the glass. They could see their babies. They wanted to feed them. But some strange invisible substance blocked the way. The birds flew about, crying in distress.

"HOO-POE! HOO-POE! HOO-POE!"

Suddenly, one of the birds flew off.

"Uh oh," Scarlett whispered to Sam. "What if the birds abandon their nest?"

"They might," said Solomon. "Birds will do that if something interferes with their nest or their nestlings. But one of the parents is still here. Let's wait and see what happens."

The second bird soon returned, carrying a banana-sized winged creature.

Sam gasped. "Scarlett, do you see what I see?"

"It looks like the bug we picked off of Grandma Mina's carpet!"

"It *is* the bug!" said Sam.

"Shhh!" said Solomon, Nathan, and B.Z. all at once.

Everyone watched to see what the hoopoes would do. The bird placed the bug in the center of the glass disk. Scarlett and Sam watched it crawl around in a circle.

CRASH! The glass shattered.

"It's the shamir! It has to be!" Scarlett cried.

"Grab it before the birds fly away with it!" Sam shouted.

Before they could get to the nest, another figure jumped up from behind the wall.

"It's mine again! Shalom, suckers!"

With the shamir gripped in his talons, Ashmodai flew off toward the desert.

CHAPTER 13
BATTLING DEMONS

"Quick! We've got to go after him!" Scarlett yelled.

"How? Ashmodai can fly," said B.Z.

"We can fly, too. We still have the carpet," Scarlett reminded them.

"But it's so slow," Nathan said.

"Maybe not," Sam replied. "The carpet was carrying a heavy load the last time we used it. There were four of us, plus water, food, and one big clay jar full of wine. That's a lot of weight."

"Plus we never really pushed the carpet to see how fast it could go," Scarlett added. "Let's give it a try."

Solomon agreed. "The twins are right. What have we got to lose?"

"Scarlett and I should go," said Sam. "We're the smallest and lightest. Every ounce counts when you need to travel fast."

"Are you sure?" B.Z. asked. "What if you have to fight demons?"

"We have our slings," Scarlett said.

"And I still have the ring," added Sam.

"If God is with you, the demons don't stand a chance," said Nathan. "I haven't gotten a message, but I do feel in my heart that you won't fail."

"Thanks, Nathan!" Scarlett and Sam said. They both hoped he was right.

***

Solomon's servants came running into the garden, carrying the carpet. They unrolled it on the lawn. Scarlett and Sam stepped aboard.

"Catch Ashmodai!" Scarlett commanded.

"Light speed!" Sam added.

"What does that mean?" Scarlett asked.

"I don't know," said Sam. "I hear it on the sci-fi channel all the time."

The carpet suddenly burst into another dimension. Time and space expanded, then contracted. Images appeared and disappeared, stretched and shrank like reflections in a fun-house mirror.

Then everything vanished in one lightning flash.

Scarlett and Sam found themselves flying over a barren landscape that looked like the surface of the moon.

"What's that up ahead?" Sam asked as soon as he recovered his voice. He pointed at a large speck surrounded by a swarm of small dots.

"Ashmodai," said Scarlett.

The king of the demons flew in the center of a swarm of demons. They looked like a collection of flying dinosaurs that had come to life. The smallest were the size of a chihuahua. The biggest were as large as airplanes. They all came fully equipped with deadly claws and fangs.

"You again?" Ashmodai snapped as soon as he saw the twins on his trail. "What do you want?"

"You know what we want, Ashmodai!" shouted Scarlett.

"Give back the shamir!" Sam yelled.

"You want it? Come get it!" He went into a long dive. The demons swarmed Scarlett and Sam from all directions.

"Battle stations!" Sam yelled. He fitted a rock to his sling and let fly. The rock caught a big demon between the eyes. The creature exploded like a balloon. But others took its place.

Scarlett nailed two more demons with her sling and knocked another off the carpet. But by now the twins were surrounded. The demons began belching out foul-smelling green smoke. Scarlett and Sam could hardly breathe. They could barely see anything through the vile green cloud. And they were running out of stones.

"We're getting hammered," Sam called to Scarlett.

Scarlett yelled back, "Use the ring!"

Sam didn't want to use the ring unless they really needed it, but they'd run out of options. Sam held up his hand and commanded, "Get these demons off our backs!" A whirling vortex of air spiraled out of the ring's clear stone. Like a mini-tornado, it pulled the demons out of the sky and swept them into the depths of the ring like table scraps being sucked down a drain.

Sam looked into the clear stone. He could see figures moving behind magical stones.

The demons were trapped inside the ring. Sam was fairly sure God's power would keep them there. Now for Ashmodai!

"Where did he go?" Scarlett asked.

"Who knows?" said Sam. "He sent those demons to distract us while he got away. He could be anywhere in the universe."

"We found him before. We'll find him again," said Scarlett. "Ready?"

"Let's go," said Sam. He held the ring to his mouth as if it were a microphone. "Take us to Ashmodai!"

The sky stretched like Silly Putty. The sun shrank to the size of an LED bulb.

They were off.

CHAPTER 14
ASHMODAI'S CAVERN

"What is this place?" Scarlett asked Sam. They found themselves in a dark, cold cavern. The only light came from the glowing rock walls, which gave off a blue flickering light—just enough for Scarlett and Sam to see a few feet ahead.

"Creepy!" Sam exclaimed. "Which way should we go? Up or down?"

"Down," said Scarlett. "It's easier."

They rolled up the carpet and carried it over

their shoulders as they proceeded down the passage. Several dark shapes came fluttering overhead. The twins jumped.

"Eek! What was that?" Scarlett yelped.

"They didn't attack us, so I don't think they were demons," said Sam, catching his breath and waiting for his heartbeat to slow down. "They're gone now. Maybe they were bats. Caves are great nesting places for bats."

"Good," said Scarlett. "Bats I can handle. I don't want to run into any more demons. Not in the dark."

Their ears gradually became attuned to the sounds around them. They heard the rush of water. That meant there was an underground stream nearby. They heard fluttering squeaks overhead. More bats. A good sign. If the cave had bats, there must be ways of getting in and out. For a bat, anyway.

There were other sounds the twins couldn't

identify. Deep grumbles and groans came from far below. They made Scarlett think of a Halloween haunted house. She wasn't a fan of haunted houses, even if they were just for fun.

Sam could tell what she was thinking. "Don't worry. The carpet got us in here. It will get us out."

Scarlett reached for Sam's hand and gave it a tight squeeze. She reminded herself of what Nathan had told them so many times. Even if they were in the darkest tunnel in the center of the earth, God could find them. God knew where they were. God would never forsake them.

Suddenly, they felt a rush of cool air. The glowing stones disappeared. Scarlett and Sam found themselves in utter darkness.

"Hello!" Sam called. His voice echoed off the cavern walls.

"I can't see a thing," Scarlett said. "This could be a problem." Without light, they might get permanently lost—or stumble into a crevasse.

Before Sam could respond, a piercing light suddenly filled the space around them. Scarlett and Sam let out a yell. They found themselves in a vast cavern the size of a football field. Immense lights set in the ceiling made the area as bright as a sports arena.

The cavern began to vibrate. The stadium lights flickered. A deep rumbling voice spoke:

"I AM ASHMODAI, KING OF THE DEMONS, RULER OF THE UNDERWORLD. WHO ARE YOU? WHY HAVE YOU COME INTO MY KINGDOM?"

The voice came from a monstrous purple head hovering high above. It looked like a prehistoric monster from a horror movie. Its eyes shot laser beams in all directions. Its jaws were like those of a gigantic crocodile, edged with sharp, curved teeth that sprayed sparks when it spoke. Its ears fanned out like an African elephant's. Its lumpy mottled skin resembled rotting fruit.

"MISERABLE WORMS! ANSWER WHEN I SPEAK TO YOU! I AM ASHMODAI, KING OF THE DEMONS," the head roared again. Its voice echoed down the cavern's tunnels and passageways.

Sam was so frightened he could hardly speak. "Unroll the carpet! Let's get out of here!"

But Scarlet wasn't scared at all. She had noticed something.

"Not so fast. We've met Ashmodai. That's not Ashmodai."

"You're right!" Sam exclaimed. "Looks like the king of the demons stole a few tricks from the Wizard of Oz."

"Or the other way around. Point is, this thing's just a talking head."

Scarlett and Sam ignored the giant head bellowing threats and began strolling around, looking into cracks and crevices, while the giant head grew angrier.

"DO YOU KNOW WHAT HAPPENS TO THOSE WHO DEFY ME? YOU WILL BE TOSSED INTO THE ENDLESS NIGHT! HORRIFYING DEMONS WILL TORMENT YOU! NO ONE CAN DEFY ME! FOR I AM ASHMODAI, RULER OF ALL!"

Sam and Scarlett peered down a staircase cut into the stone floor. At the bottom, facing a video screen on the wall, stood Ashmodai. The talking head was on the screen, jabbering away, while Ashmodai pushed buttons on a keyboard and moved a mouse around as he spoke into a microphone. Clearly, the demon king was ahead of his time in the technology department.

"Hey there," said the twins.

Ashmodai spun around. "Go away!" he said. "You're not supposed to see this."

"Well, we did. Why don't you cut the nonsense and let's talk business?" said Scarlett.

Sam jumped in. "We want the shamir back.

You had no right to take it. Solomon needs it to build the Temple. So hand it over."

"I don't think so," Ashmodai said. He opened his talons. The shamir rested in the palm of his hand.

"I've been having a lot of fun with this little guy," Ashmodai said. "He's amazing. You move him over the hardest rock and it splits in two. How do you like my condo? This was just an ordinary cave when I began fixing it up with the help of the shamir. And I'm far from done. I'm gonna put in a hot tub, sauna, game room . . . but I'm way behind. Everything had to stop when God took the shamir away. I'm not giving it back now. Tell Solomon to check back with me in a couple of centuries. Maybe I'll be finished by then."

"You're finished now," said Sam. He pointed Solomon's ring at Ashmodai. The demons inside the stone began squeaking and peeping in the presence of their master. "Hand over the shamir—unless you'd like to join your pals inside the ring!"

Ashmodai's fist closed around the creature. He glared at Sam. "Not so fast. You make one move with that ring and I squash this little bug. That'll be the end of the shamir and the end of your Temple!"

Sam lowered his hand. "Okay, Ashmodai. Maybe we can work out a deal. We want the shamir. What do you want in return?"

"What are you talking about, Sam?" Scarlett hissed. "You don't make deals with demons!"

"You do what you have to do," Sam told her. "Come on, Ashmodai. I'm listening."

"Hmm! I like your style, kid. You've got a bit of demon in you. Tell you what I'll do. I'll trade you the shamir for . . . Solomon's ring! How about it?" Ashmodai said.

"No!" Scarlett shouted at Sam. "Don't even consider it! You can't give power like that to the king of the demons. He'll use it to enslave the world . . . if he doesn't destroy it!"

"Don't listen to her, Sam," Ashmodai said, his voice reasonable and soothing. "This is a fair trade."

"I need to think about this," Sam said.

"Take your time," said Ashmodai. "I have plenty of time. Eons and eons."

Scarlett pulled at Sam's arm. "No, Sam! I can't let you do this!"

Sam shrugged her off. "Leave me alone, Scarlett. You can't tell me what to do. I've made up my mind. Okay, Ashmodai. It's a deal. The ring for the shamir. Let's do it."

Ashmodai's grin showed every one of his fangs. "Smart boy. I knew you'd come around." He held out both hands. The left was empty. The right held the shamir. Sam took the shamir as he placed Solomon's ring in Ashmodai's empty hand.

Scarlett couldn't stop herself from crying out. "Oh, no! Sam! What have you done?"

"It's all mine! I own the universe!" Ashmodai crowed as he slipped the ring onto his finger. Or tried to. He twisted, pushed, jammed the ring against his knuckle. It wouldn't go on. It didn't fit.

"I'll have to grease it," Ashmodai muttered.

"Grease it all you want. It still won't go on. Nothing can make it go on," said Sam.

"Whaaat?" Ashmodai exclaimed.

"I never had the power to give the ring away. No one can give it away," Sam told him. "The ring chooses who can wear it. It has to be someone worthy, someone who will use it for a good cause. It definitely won't choose you, Ashmodai. You may as well give it back."

"No!" Ashmodai's enraged roar echoed in the upper reaches of the cavern. "You cheated me!"

"He did not," said Scarlett, smiling through tears of joy. "You stole the shamir. It wasn't yours to begin with. Now we have it back and our business with you is done."

Sam held out his hand. "Ring, come back." The ring flew from Ashmodai's hands and fixed itself on Sam's finger. "Have a nice day, Ashmodai. Enjoy your man cave."

Scarlett unrolled the carpet, and the twins hopped on. "Solomon's palace!" Scarlett shouted. "Full speed!"

CHAPTER 15

KNIGHTS OF THE LION OF JUDAH

Solomon's voice rang out over the thousands of people assembled in the palace courtyard. Thousands more filled the streets, balconies, and rooftops of Jerusalem to see the ceremony. "We are assembled here to pay tribute to two of the bravest heroes in Israel's history!" the king began.

A week had passed since Scarlett and Sam had returned to Jerusalem with the shamir. Work on the Temple had already begun. The city's best stonecutters were so excited to work with the shamir that they'd volunteered for the job. Solomon would pay them once the treasury got up and running again. And Solomon had managed to get the trapped demons out of his ring and had roped them into working on the construction crew. Hauling the finished stones and setting them in place was one way for them to make up for all the mischief they'd done over the centuries.

Now, Scarlett and Sam stood with Solomon, B.Z., and Nathan on the Queen of Sheba's flying carpet as it hovered above the crowd. The twins couldn't help noticing the change in Solomon. Despite his threadbare robe and his awkwardly fitting crown, he stood tall and held his head high. He finally looked like a real king.

"What are we supposed to do?" Sam asked his sister.

"I think we're supposed to bow," Scarlett said.

Scarlett and Sam bowed the way they had seen people do it in movies. Scarlett wondered if she should attempt a curtsy, but decided against it. Without practice, she was liable to fall off the carpet.

Solomon stopped them in mid-bow. "No. You shall not bow to me or anyone. Scarlett and Sam, you have done a great service to the Jewish people. You found the shamir, which had been lost for centuries. You defeated the king of the demons. You made possible the building of our Holy Temple. The people of Israel will be in your debt for generations to come."

Sam blushed. Scarlett looked at her shoes, trying to hide her embarrassment. "We were glad to help you out," she murmured.

"And we couldn't have done anything without B.Z. and Nathan," Sam added.

"There's someone else we all need to thank," said B.Z.

Nathan agreed. "We owe everything to God."

"And we do thank God, every day," Solomon agreed. "But today I wish to give special thanks to our friends Scarlett and Sam."

Solomon hung a gold medal around each twin's neck. On the front was the six-pointed Star of David. On the back, a roaring lion standing on his hind legs.

"As King of Israel, I welcome Scarlett and Sam into the Noble Order of the Lion of Judah."

The thousands of people in the courtyard, in the streets, and on the rooftops cheered.

"It's a privilege, Solomon," the twins said.

Solomon smiled at them as he stepped off the carpet onto the balcony below. "You taught me the true meaning of wisdom. A wise person is not someone who thinks he or she knows everything. A truly wise person knows how to ask the right questions and whom to call on for answers."

B.Z. joined Solomon on the balcony. "Scarlett and Sam, I have been in a hundred battles. Yet you've taught me the true meaning of courage. A hero is not someone without fear. It is someone who faces danger despite fear and does what needs to be done."

Nathan took his turn. "You both taught me something, too. God speaks to all of us in different ways. I hear a voice. But God also sends ideas. God sends courage. God sends faith in times of trouble. God truly speaks to us all. We just need to listen."

Nathan hopped down to the balcony, leaving the twins standing alone on the carpet, at a loss for words.

Scarlett cleared her throat. "I really don't know what to say except . . ."

Just then, the carpet began to lift. "Guess this is our cue to exit," said Sam. He and Scarlett waved to their friends just before the carpet whisked them away from the palace. It circled above Jerusalem, passed over the Temple Mount, and rose high into the clouds.

***

"Scarlett! Sam! What have you done?"

The twins looked around. They were back in the dining room, and one look at Grandma Mina's face told them something was wrong. The carpet hung in its usual place on the wall. It looked the same as before. But one glance at the table revealed the problem. The glass jar that had held the strange bug lay shattered to bits.

"I told you to take that bug outside!" Grandma Mina yelled. "It gotten out and now it's loose again. You'd better find it before I do."

Sam looked at Scarlett. "There's only one kind of bug that could shatter a glass jar."

Scarlett grinned. "Don't worry, Grandma. We'll clean up the glass. And you don't have to be scared of the bug. I have a feeling it won't be back."

"Wise words," Sam whispered. "I'll bet Solomon would be proud."

Author's Note

Creating this adventure for Scarlett and Sam gave me an opportunity to revisit one of my favorite stories, the legend of King Solomon and the shamir.

The legend of the shamir is a midrash. Midrashim are stories or teachings that explain or expand the Torah text. The earliest go back to the 2nd century CE. The stories themselves are much older. The legend of the shamir explains how King Solomon was able to shape the huge stones of the Temple without using iron tools.

Solomon's Temple was destroyed by Babylonian invaders in 586 BCE. The Hebrew people rebuilt the Temple in 515 BCE, and King Herod later expanded it to create the Second Temple. By all accounts, it was one of the wonders of the world. This magnificent Temple stood until 70 CE, when it was destroyed by the Romans. Later generations marveled at the huge remaining stones of the Kotel, the Western Wall. They believed that only demons could have shaped such immense blocks and moved them into place. That may have been how Ashmodai, king of the demons, entered the story.

The traditional Jewish view of demons and spirits—as well as other "evils" such as disease-causing bacteria and viruses—is that God created them to fulfill some purpose. In other words, everything that exists comes from God.